El patito feo
The Ugly Duckling

Adaptación / *Adaptation:* Luz Orihuela

Ilustraciones / *Illustrations:* Irene Bordoy

Traducción / *Translation:* Esther Sarfatti

SCHOLASTIC INC.

New York   Toronto   London   Auckland   Sydney
Mexico City   New Delhi   Hong Kong   Buenos Aires

En la orilla del lago hay mucho alboroto.

¿Qué pasa?

There's a lot of noise at the lake.

What's going on?

2

Los patitos han salido de los huevos.

Son todos iguales y ¡tan bonitos!

The ducklings have hatched!

They all look alike!

They're so cute!

¿Todos iguales?

¡Nooo! Hay uno distinto.

Do they all look alike?

Nooo! There's one that is different.

—¡Vete! —le dicen los otros—. ¿No ves que
no eres como nosotros?

"Go away!" say the other ducklings.
"You don't look like us."

 8

El patito está muy, muy triste. Sabe bien

que es diferente.

The duckling is very, very sad.

He looks different from the others.

—¿Han visto lo lindos que son los patitos? —dicen todos los animales—. Todos son lindos menos uno.

"Have you seen the adorable ducklings?" ask the animals.
"They're all so cute. Except one."

Y el patito se encuentra cada vez más solo

y cada vez más triste.

The ugly duckling feels very lonely and very sad.

—Pero ¿qué gritos son esos? ¿Por qué tanto ruido? —dice el patito desde su rincón.

"What's all that noise?" asks the ugly duckling.

—¡Ven! —lo llama un grupo de cisnes blancos

muy elegantes—.

Mira, eres como nosotros.

"Come to us!"

The ugly duckling sees a group of beautiful white swans.

"You look like us!" they say.

Y, claro, el patito se fue con ellos. Ahora sí que es feliz.

Of course, the duckling swam to them. Now he's happy.

A la orilla del lago vuelve la calma y la armonía.

At the lake, it is calm once again.

ISBN-13: 978-0-439-77376-8
ISBN-10: 0-439-77376-8

Illustrations copyright © 2003 by Irene Bordoy
Text copyright © 2003 by Combel Editorial, S.A.
English translation copyright © 2006 by Scholastic Inc.
All rights reserved. Published by Scholastic Inc., 557 Broadway, New York, NY 10012,
by arrangement with Combel Editorial.
SCHOLASTIC and associated logos are trademarks and/or registered trademarks of Scholastic Inc.

12 11 10 9 8 7   9 10 11 12/0

Printed in China   67

First Scholastic bilingual printing, February 2006